THE JUMPING FROG

and other
stories
by
Mark Twain

With Illustrations from the hand
of Mr. Donald McKay

PETER PAUPER PRESS, INC.
WHITE PLAINS • NEW YORK

THE CONTENTS

THE JUMPING FROG OF CALAVERAS COUNTY

Even a criminal is entitled to fair play; and certainly when a man who has done no harm has been unjustly treated, he is privileged to do his best to right himself. My attention has just been called to an article some three years old in a French Magazine entitled, "Revue des Deux Mondes" (Review of Some Two Worlds), wherein the writer treats of "Les Humoristes Americaines" (These Humorists Americans). I am one of these humorists Americans dissected by him, and hence the complaint I am making.

This gentleman's article is an able one (as articles go, in the French, where they always tangle up everything to that degree that when you start into a sentence you never know whether you are going to come out alive or not). It is a very good article, and the writer says all manner of kind and complimentary things about me — for which I am sure I thank him with all my heart; but then why should he go and spoil all his praise by one unlucky experiment? What I refer to is this: he says my Jumping Frog is a funny story, but still he can't see why it should ever really convulse anyone with laughter — and straightway proceeds to translate it into French in order to prove to his nation that there is nothing so very extravagantly funny about it. Just there is where my complaint originates. He has not translated it at all; he has simply mixed it all up; it is no more like the Jumping Frog when he gets through with it than I am like a meridian of longitude. In order that even the unlettered may know my injury and give me their compassion, I have been at infinite pains and trouble to retranslate this French version back into English; and to tell the truth I have well nigh worn myself out at it, having scarcely rested from my work during five days and nights.

I cannot speak the French language, but I can translate very well, though not fast, I being self-educated. I ask the reader to run his eye over the original English version of the Jumping Frog, and then read my retranslation from the French, and kindly take notice how the Frenchman has riddled the grammar. I think it is the worst I ever saw; and yet the French are called a polished nation. If I had a boy that put sentences together as they do, I would polish him to some purpose. Without further introduction, the Jumping Frog, as I originally wrote it, was as follows — [after it will be found my retranslation from the French]:

THE NOTORIOUS JUMPING FROG OF CALAVERAS COUNTY

IN COMPLIANCE with the request of a friend of mine, who wrote me from the East, I called on good-natured, garrulous old Simon

Wheeler, and inquired after my friend's friend, Leonidas W. Smiley, as requested to do, and I hereunto append the result. I have a lurking suspicion that *Leonidas W.* Smiley is a myth; that my friend never knew such a personage; and that he only conjectured that if I asked old Wheeler about him, it would remind him of his infamous *Jim* Smiley, and he would go to work and bore me to death with some exasperating reminiscence of him as long and as tedious as it should be useless to me. If that was the design, it succeeded.

I found Simon Wheeler dozing comfortably by the bar-room stove of the dilapidated tavern in the decayed mining camp of Angel's, and I noticed that he was fat and bald-headed, and had an expression of winning gentleness and simplicity upon his tranquil countenance. He roused up, and gave me good-day. I told him a friend of mine had commissioned me to make some inquiries about a cherished companion of his boyhood named *Leonidas W.* Smiley — *Rev. Leonidas W.* Smiley, a young minister of the Gospel, who he had heard was at one time a resident of Angel's Camp. I added that if Mr. Wheeler could tell me anything about this Rev. Leonidas W. Smiley, I would feel under many obligations to him.

Simon Wheeler backed me into a corner and blockaded me there with his chair, and then sat down and reeled off the monotonous narrative which follows this paragraph. He never smiled, he never frowned, he never changed his voice from the gentle-flowing key to which he tuned his initial sentence, he never betrayed the slightest suspicion of enthusiasm; but all through the interminable narrative there ran a vein of impressive earnestness and sincerity, which showed me plainly that, so far from his imagining that there was anything ridiculous or funny about his story, he regarded it as a really important matter, and admired its two heroes as men of transcendent genius in *finesse*. I let him go on in his own way, and never interrupted him once.

REV. LEONIDAS W. H'm, Reverend Le —well, there was a feller here once by the name of *Jim* Smiley, in the winter of '49 — or may be it was the spring of '50 — I don't recollect exactly, somehow, though what makes me think it was one or the other is because I remember the big flume warn't finished when he first came to the camp; but any way, he was the curiosest man about always betting on anything that turned up you ever see, if he could get anybody to bet on the other side; and if he couldn't he'd change sides. Any way that suited the other man would suit *him* — any way just so's he got a bet, *he* was satisfied. But still he was lucky, uncommon lucky; he most always come out winner. He was always ready and laying for a chance; there couldn't be no solit'ry thing mentioned but that feller'd offer to bet on it, and take ary side you please, as I was just telling you. If there was a horse-race, you'd find him flush or you'd find him busted at the end of it; if there was a dog-fight, he'd bet on it; if there was a cat-fight, he'd bet on it; if there was a chicken-fight, he'd bet on it; why if there was two birds setting on a fence, he would bet you which one would fly first; or if there was a camp-meeting, he would be there reg'lar to bet on Parson Walker, which he judged to be the best exhorter about here, and so he was too, and a good man. If he even see a straddle-bug start to go anywheres, he would bet you how long it would take him to get to — to wherever he was going to, and if you took him up, he would foller that straddle-bug to Mexico but what he would find out where he was bound for and how long he was on the road. Lots of the boys here has seen that Smiley and can tell you about him. Why, it never made no difference to *him* — he'd bet on *any* thing — the dangest feller. Parson Walker's wife laid very sick once, for a good while, and it seemed as if they warn't going to save her; but one morning he come in, and Smiley up and asked him how she was, and he said she was considerable better — thank the Lord for his inf'nit mercy — and coming on so smart that with the blessing of Prov'dence she'd get well yet; and Smiley, before he thought, says, "Well, I'll risk two-and-a-half she don't anyway."

Thish-yer Smiley had a mare — the boys

called her the fifteen-minute nag, but that was only in fun, you know, because of course she was faster than that — and he used to win money on that horse, for all she was so slow and always had the asthma, or the distemper, or the consumption, or something of that kind. They used to give her two or three hundred yards start, and then pass her under way; but always at the fag-end of the race she'd get excited and desperate-like, and come cavorting and straddling up, and scattering her legs around limber, sometimes in the air, and sometimes out to one side amongst the fences, and kicking up m-o-r-e dust and raising m-o-r-e racket with her coughing and sneezing and blowing her nose — and *always* fetch up at the stand just about a neck ahead, as near as you could cipher it down.

And he had a little small bull-pup, that to look at him you'd think he warn't worth a cent but to set around and look ornery and lay for a chance to steal something. But as soon as money was up on him he was a different dog; his under-jaw'd begin to stick out like the fo'-castle of a steamboat, and his teeth would uncover and shine like the furnaces. And a dog might tackle him and bully-rag him, and bite him, and throw him over his shoulder two or three times, and Andrew Jackson — which was the name of the pup — Andrew Jackson would never let on but what *he* was satisfied, and hadn't expected nothing else — and the bets being double and doubled on the other side all the time, till the money was all up; and then all of a sudden he would grab that other dog jest by the j'int of his hind leg and freeze to it — not chaw, you understand, but only just grip and hang on till they throwed up the sponge, if it was a year. Smiley always come out winner on that pup, till he harnessed a dog once that didn't have no hind legs, because they'd been sawed off in a circular saw, and when the thing had gone along far enough, and the money was all up, and he come to make a snatch for his pet holt, he see in a minute how he'd been imposed on, and how the other dog had him in the door, so to speak, and he 'peared surprised, and then he looked sorter discouraged-like, and didn't try no more to win the fight, and so he got shucked out bad. He gave Smiley a look, as much as to say his heart was broke, and it was *his* fault, for putting up a dog that hadn't no hind legs for him to take holt of, which was his main dependence in a fight, and then he limped off a piece and laid down and died. It was a good pup, was that Andrew Jackson, and would have made a name for hisself if he'd lived, for the stuff was in him and he had genius — I know it, because he hadn't no opportunities to speak of, and it don't stand to reason that a dog could make such a fight as he could under them circumstances if he hadn't no talent. It always makes me feel sorry when I think of that last fight of his'n, and the way it turned out.

Well, thish-yer Smiley had rat-tarriers, and chicken cocks, and tom-cats and all of them kind of things, till you couldn't rest, and you couldn't fetch nothing for him to bet on but he'd match you. He ketched a frog one day, and took him home, and said he cal'lated to educate him; and so he never done nothing for three months but set in his back yard and learn that frog to jump. And you bet you he *did* learn him, too. He'd give him a little punch behind, and the next minute you'd see that frog whirling in the air like a doughnut — see him turn one summerset, or may be a couple, if he got a good start, and come down flat-footed and all right, like a cat. He got him up so in the matter of ketching flies, and kep' him in practice so constant, that he'd nail a fly every time as fur as he could see him. Smiley said all a frog wanted was education, and he could do 'most anything — and I believe him. Why, I've seen him set Dan'l Webster down here on this floor — Dan'l Webster was the name of the frog — and sing out, "Flies, Dan'l, flies!" and quicker'n you could wink he'd spring straight up and snake a fly off'n the counter there, and flop down on the floor ag'in as solid as a gob of mud, and fall to scratching the side of his head with his hind foot as indifferent as if he hadn't no idea he'd been doin' any more'n any frog might do. You never see a frog so modest and straightfor'ard as he was, for all he was so gifted. And when it come to fair and square jumping on a dead level, he could get over more ground at one straddle than any animal of his breed you ever see. Jumping on a dead level was his strong suit, you understand; and when it come to that, Smiley would ante up money on him as long as he had a red. Smiley was monstrous proud of his frog, and well he might be, for fellers that had traveled and been everywheres, all said he laid over any frog that ever *they* see.

Well, Smiley kep' the beast in a little lattice box, and he used to fetch him down town sometimes and lay for a bet. One day a feller — a stranger in the camp, he was — come acrost him with his box, and says:

"What might it be that you've got in the box?"

And Smiley says, sorter indifferent-like, "It might be a parrot, or it might be a canary, maybe, but it ain't — it's only just a frog."

And the feller took it, and looked at it careful, and turned it round this way and that, and says, "H'm — so 'tis. Well, what's *he* good for?"

"Well," Smiley says, easy and careless, "he's good enough for *one* thing, I should judge — he can outjump any frog in Calaveras county."

The feller took the box again, and took another long, particular look, and give it back to Smiley, and says, very deliberate, "Well," he says, "I don't see no p'ints about that frog that's any better'n any other frog."

"Maybe you don't," Smiley says. "Maybe you understand frogs and maybe you don't understand 'em; maybe you've had experience, and maybe you ain't only a amature, as it were. Anyways, I've got *my* opinion and I'll risk forty dollars that he can outjump any frog in Calaveras county."

And the feller studied a minute, and then says, kinder sad like, "Well, I'm only a stranger here, and I ain't got no frog; but if I had a frog, I'd bet you."

And then Smiley says, "That's all right — that's all right — if you'll hold my box a minute, I'll go and get you a frog." And so the feller took the frog, and put up his forty dollars along with Smiley's and set down to wait.

So he set there a good while thinking and thinking to hisself, and then he got the frog out and prized his mouth open and took a teaspoon and filled him full of quail shot — filled him pretty near up to his chin — and set him on the floor. Smiley he went to the swamp and slopped around in the mud for a long time, and finally he ketched a frog, and fetched him in, and give him to this feller, and says:

"Now, if you're ready, set him along side of Dan'l, with his forepaws just even with Dan'l's, and I'll give the word." Then he says, "One — two — three — *git!*" and him and the feller touched up the frogs from behind, and the new frog hopped off lively, but Dan'l give a heave, and hysted up his shoulders — so — like a Frenchman, but it warn't no use — he couldn't budge; he was planted as solid as a church, and he couldn't no more stir than if he was anchored out. Smiley was a good deal surprised, and he was disgusted too, but he didn't have no idea what the matter was, of course.

The feller took the money and started away; and when he was going out at the door, he sorter jerked his thumb over his shoulder — so — at Dan'l, and says again, very deliberate, "Well," he says, "I don't see no p'ints about that frog that's any better'n any other frog."

Smiley he stood scratching his head and looking down at Dan'l a long time, and at last he says, "I do wonder what in the nation that frog throwed off for — I wonder if there ain't something the matter with him — he 'pears to look mighty baggy, somehow." And he ketched Dan'l by the nap of the neck, and hefted him, and says, "Why blame my cats if he don't weigh five pounds!" and turned him upside down and he belched out a double handful of shot. And then he see how it was, and he was the maddest man — he set the frog down and took out after that feller, but he never ketched him. And —"

[Here Simon Wheeler heard his name called from the front yard, and got up to see what was wanted.] And turning to me as he moved away, he said: "Just set where you are, stranger, and

15

rest easy — I ain't going to be gone a second."

But, by your leave, I did not think that a continuation of the history of the enterprising vagabond *Jim* Smiley would be likely to afford me much information concerning the Rev. *Lionidas W.* Smiley, and so I started away.

At the door I met the sociable Wheeler returning, and he buttonholed me and recommenced:

"Well, thish-yer Smiley had a yaller one-eyed cow that didn't have no tail, only just a short stump like a bannanner, and —"

However, lacking both time and inclination, I did not wait to hear about the afflicted cow, but took my leave.

[Translation of the above back from the French]

THE FROG JUMPING OF THE COUNTY OF CALAVERAS

IT THERE was one time here an individual known under the name of Jim Smiley: it was in the winter of '49, possibly well at the spring of '50, I no me recollect not exactly. This which me makes to believe that it was the one or the other, it is that I shall remember that the grand flume is not achieved when he arrives at the camp for the first time, but of all sides he was the man the most fond of to bet which one have seen, betting upon all that which is presented, when he could find an adversary; and when he

16

not of it could not, he passed to the side opposed. All that which convenienced to the other, to him convenienced also; seeing that he had a bet, Smiley was satisfied. And he had a chance! a chance even worthless: nearly always he gained. It must to say that he was always near to himself expose, but one no could mention the least thing without that this gaillard offered to bet the bottom, no matter what, and to take the side that one him would, as I you it said all at the hour (tout a l'heure). If it there was of races, you him find rich or ruined at the end; if it there is a combat of dogs, he bring his bet; he himself laid always for a combat of cats, for a combat of cocks; — by-blue! if you have see two birds upon a fence, he you should have offered of to bet which of those birds shall fly the first; and if there is *meeting* at the camp (*meeting* au camp) he comes to bet regularly for the cure Walker, which he judged to be the best predicator of the neighborhood (predicateur des environs) and which he was in effect, and a brave man. He would encounter a bug of wood in the road, whom he will bet upon the time which he shall take to go where she would go — and if you him have take at the word, he will follow the bug as far as Mexique, without himself caring to go so far; neither of the time which he there lost. One time the woman of the cure Walker is very sick during long time, it seemed that one not her saved not; but one morning the cure arrives,

17

and Smiley him demanded how she goes, and he said that she is well better, grace to the infinite misery (lui demande comment elle va, et il dit qu'elle est bien mieux, grace a l'infinie misericorde) so much better that with the benediction of the Providence she herself of it would pull out (elle s'en tirerait); and behold without there thinking Smiley responds: "Well, I gage two-and-half that she will die all of same."

This Smiley had an animal which the boys called the nag of the quarter of hour, but solely for pleasantry, you comprehend, because, well understand, she was more fast as that! [Now why that exclamation? — M.T.] And it was custom of to gain of the silver with this beast, notwithstanding she was poussive, cornarde, always taken of asthma, of colics or of consumption, or something of approaching. One him would give two or three hundred yards at the departure, then one him passed without pain; but never at the last she not fail of herself echauffer, of herself exasperate, and she arrives herself ecartant, se defendant, her legs greles in the air before the obstacles, sometimes them elevating and making with this more of dust than any horse, more of noise above with his eternumens and reniflemens — crac! she arrives then always first by one head, as just as one can it measure. And he had a small bull dog (boule dogue!) who, to him see, no value, not a cent; one would believe that to bet against him it was to steal, so much he was ordinary; but as soon as the game made, she becomes another dog. Her jaw inferior commence to project like a deck of before, his teeth themselves discover brilliant like some furnaces, and a dog could him tackle (le taquiner), him excite, him murder (le mordre), him throw two or three times over his shoulder, Andre Jackson — this was the name of the dog — Andre Jackson takes that tranquilly, as if he not himself was never expecting other thing, and when the bets were doubled and redoubled against him, he you seize the other dog just at the articulation of the leg of behind, and he not it leave more, not that he it masticate, you conceive, but he himself there shall be holding during until that one throws the sponge in the air, must he wait a year. Smiley gained always with this beast-la; unhappily they have finished by elevating a dog who no had not of feet of behind, because one them had sawed; and when things were at the point that he would, and that he came to himself throw upon his morsel favorite, the poor dog comprehended in an instant that he himself was deceived in him, and that the other dog him had. You no have never see person having the air more penaud and more discouraged; he not made no effort to gain the combat, and was rudely shucked.

Eh Bien! this Smiley nourished some terriers a rats, and some cocks of combat, and some cats, and all sorts of things; and with his rage of betting one no had more of repose. He trapped one day a frog and him imported with him (et l'emporta chez lui) saying that he pretended to make his education. You me believe if you will, but during three months he not has nothing done but to him apprehend to jump (apprendre a sauter) in a court retired of her mansion (de sa maison). And I you respond that he have succeeded. He him gives a small blow by behind, and the instant after you shall see the frog turn in the air like a grease-biscuit, make one summersault, sometimes two, when she was well started, and re-fall upon his feet like a cat. He him had accomplished in the art of to gobble the flies (gober les mouches), and him there exercised continually — so well that a fly at the most far that she appeared was a fly lost. Smiley had custom to say that all which lacked to a frog it was the education, but with the education she could do nearly all — and I him believe. Tenez, I him have seen pose Daniel Webster thereupon this plank — Daniel Webster was the name of the frog — and to him sing, "Some flies, Daniel, some flies!" — in the flash of the eye Daniel had bounded and seized a fly here upon the encounter, then jumped anew at the earth, where he rested truly to himself scratch the head with his behind-foot, as if he no had not the least idea of his superiority. Never you not have seen frog as modest, as natural, sweet as she was. And when he himself agitated to jump purely and simply upon plain earth, she does more ground in one jump than any beast of his species than you can know. To jump plain — this was his strong. When he himself agitated for that, Smiley multiplied the bets upon her as long as there to him remained a red. It must to know, Smiley was monstrously proud of his frog, and he of it was right, for some men who were traveled, who had all seen, said that they to him would be injurious to him compare to another frog. Smiley guarded Daniel in a little box latticed which he carried bytimes to the village for some bet.

One day an individual stranger at the camp him arrested with his box and him said:

"What is this that you have then shut up there within?"

Smiley said, with an air indifferent:

"That could be a paroquet, or a syringe (ou un serin), but this no is nothing of such, it not is but a frog."

The individual it took, it regarded with care, it turned from one side and from the other, then he said:

"Tiens! in effect! — At what is she good?"

"My God!" respond Smiley, always with an air disengaged, "she is good for one thing, to my notice, (a mon avis), she can batter in jumping (elle peut batter en sautant) all frogs of the county of Calaveras."

The individual re-took the box, it examined

21

of new longly, and it rendered to Smiley in saying with an air deliberate:

"Eh bien! I no saw not that that frog had nothing of better than each frog." (Je ne vois pas que cette grenouille ait rien de mieux qu'aucune grenouille). [If that isn't grammar gone to seed, then I count myself no judge. — M.T.]

"Possible that you not it saw not," said Smiley, "possible that you — you comprehend frogs; possible that you not you there comprehend nothing; possible that you had of the experience, and possible that you not be but an amateur. Of all manner, (De toute maniere) I bet forty dollars that she batter in jumping no matter which frog of the county of Calaveras."

The individual reflected a second, and said like sad:

"I not am but a stranger here, I no have not a frog; but if I of it had one, I would embrace the bet."

"Strong well!" respond Smiley; "nothing of more facility. If you will hold my box a minute, I go you to search a frog (j'irai vous chercher)."

Behold, then, the individual, who guards the box, who puts his forty dollars upon those of Smiley, and who attends, (et qui attend). He attended enough longtimes, reflecting all solely. And figure you that he takes Daniel, him opens the mouth by force and with a tea-spoon him fills with shot of the hunt, even him fills just to the chin, then he him puts by the earth.

Smiley during these times was at slopping in a swamp. Finally he trapped (attrape) a frog, him carried to that individual, and said:

"Now if you be ready, put him all against Daniel, with their before-feet upon the same line, and I give the signal" — then he added: "One, two, three, — advance!"

Him and the individual touched their frogs by behind, and the frog new put to jump smartly, but Daniel himself lifted ponderously, exalted the shoulders, thus, like a Frenchman — to what good? he not could budge, he is planted solid like a church, he not advance no more than if one him had put at the anchor.

Smiley was surprised and disgusted, but he not himself doubted not of the turn being intended (mais il ne se doutait pas du tour, bien entendu). The individual empocketed the silver, himself with it went, and of it himself in going is it that he no gives not a jerk of thumb over the shoulder — like that — at the poor Daniel, in saying with his air deliberate — (L'individu empoche l'argent, s'en va et en s'en allant est ce qu'il ne donne pas un coup de pouce pardessus l'epaule, comme ca, au pauvre Daniel, en disant de son air delibere):

"Eh bien! I *no see not that that frog has nothing better than another.*"

Smiley himself scratched longtimes the head, the eyes fixed upon Daniel, until that which at last he said:

"I me demand how the devil it makes itself that this beast has refused. Is it that she had something? One would believe that she is stuffed."

He grasped Daniel by the skin of the neck, him lifted and said:

"The wolf me bite if he no weigh not five pounds."

He him reversed and the unhappy belched two handfuls of shot (et le malhereux, etc.) — When Smiley recognized how it was, he was like mad. He deposited his frog by the earth and ran after that individual, but he not him caught never.

Such is the Jumping Frog, to the distorted French eye. I claim that I never put together such an odious mixture of bad grammar and delirium tremens in my life. And what has a poor foreigner like me done, to be abused and misrepresented like this? When I say, "Well, I don't see no p'ints about that frog that's any better'n any other frog," is it kind, is it just, for this Frenchman to try to make it appear that I said: "Eh bien! I no saw that that frog had nothing of better than each frog?" I have no heart to write more. I never felt so about any-thing before.

TAMING THE BICYCLE

I thought the matter over, and concluded I could do it. So I went down and bought a barrel of Pond's Extract and a bicycle. The Expert came home with me to instruct me. We chose the back yard, for the sake of privacy, and went to work.

Mine was not a full-grown bicycle, but only a colt — a fifty-inch, with the pedals shortened up to forty-eight — and skittish, like any other colt. The Expert explained the thing's points briefly, then he got on its back and rode around a little, to show me how easy it was to do. He said that the dismounting was perhaps the hardest thing to learn, and so we would leave that to the last. But he was in error there. He found, to his surprise and joy, that all that he needed to do was to get me on to the machine and stand out of the way; I could get off, myself. Although I was wholly inexperienced, I dismounted in the best time on record. He was on that side, shoving up the machine; we all came down with a crash, he at the bottom, I next, and the machine on top.

We examined the machine, but it was not in the least injured. This was hardly believable. Yet the Expert assured me that it was true; in fact, the examination proved it. I was partly to realize, then, how admirably these things are constructed. We applied some Pond's Extract, and resumed. The Expert got on the *other* side to shove up this time, but I dismounted on that side; so the result was as before.

The machine was not hurt. We oiled ourselves up again, and resumed. This time the Expert took up a sheltered position behind, but somehow or other we landed on him again.

He was full of surprised admiration; said it

was abnormal. She was all right, not a scratch on her, not a timber started anywhere. I said it was wonderful, while we were greasing up, but he said that when I came to know these steel spider-webs I would realize that nothing but dynamite could cripple them. Then he limped out to position, and we resumed once more. This time the Expert took up the position of short-stop, and got a man to shove up behind. We got up a handsome speed, and presently traversed a brick, and I went out over the top of the tiller and landed, head down, on the instructor's back, and saw the machine fluttering in the air between me and the sun. It was well it came down on us, for that broke the fall, and it was not injured.

Five days later I got out and was carried down to the hospital, and found the Expert doing pretty fairly. In a few more days I was quite sound. I attribute this to my prudence in always dismounting on something soft. Some recommend a feather bed, but I think an Expert is better.

The Expert got out at last, brought four assistants with him. It was a good idea. These four held the graceful cobweb upright while I climbed into the saddle; then they formed in column and marched on either side of me while the Expert pushed behind; all hands assisted at the dismount.

The bicycle had what is called the "wabbles,"

and had them very badly. In order to keep my position, a good many things were required of me, and in every instance the thing required was against nature. Against nature, but not against the *laws* of nature. That is to say, that whatever the needed thing might be, my nature, habit, and breeding moved me to attempt it in one way, while some immutable and unsuspected law of physics required that it be done in just the other way. I perceived by this how radically and grotesquely wrong had been the lifelong education of my body and members. They were steeped in ignorance; they knew nothing — nothing which it could profit them to know. For instance, if I found myself falling to the right, I put the tiller hard down the other way, by a quite natural impulse, and so violated a law, and kept on going down. The law required the opposite thing — the big wheel must be turned in the direction in which you are falling. It is hard to believe this, when you are told it. And not merely hard to believe it, but impossible; it is opposed to all your notions. And it is just as hard to do it, after you do come to believe it. Believing it, and knowing by the most convincing proof that it is true, does not help it: you can't any more *do* it than you could before; you can neither force nor persuade yourself to do it at first. The intellect has to come to the front, now. It has to teach the limbs to discard their old education and adopt the new.

The steps of one's progress are distinctly marked. At the end of each lesson he knows he has acquired something, and he also knows what that something is, and likewise that it will stay with him. It is not like studying German, where you mull along, in a groping, uncertain way, for thirty years; and at last, just as you think you've got it, they spring the subjunctive on you, and there you are. No — and I see now, plainly enough, that the great pity about the German language is, that you can't fall off it and hurt yourself. There is nothing like that feature to make you attend strictly to business. But I also see, by what I have learned of bicycling, that the right and only sure way to learn German is by the bicycling method. That is to say, take a grip on one villainy of it at a time, and learn it — not ease up and shirk to the next, leaving that one half learned.

When you have reached the point in bicycling where you can balance the machine tolerably fairly and propel it and steer it, then comes your next task — how to mount it. You do it in this way: you hop along behind it on your right foot, resting the other on the mounting-peg, and grasping the tiller with your hands. At the word, you rise on the peg, stiffen your left leg, hang your other one around in the air in a general and indefinite way, lean your stomach against the rear of the saddle, and then fall off, maybe on one side, maybe on the other; but you fall off. You get up and do it again; and once more; and then several times.

By this time you have learned to keep your balance; and also to steer without wrenching the tiller out by the roots (I say tiller because it *is* a tiller; "handle-bar" is a lamely descriptive phrase). So you steer along, straight ahead, a little while, then you rise forward, with a steady strain, bringing your right leg, and then your body, into the saddle, catch your breath, fetch a violent hitch this way and then that, and down you go again.

But you have ceased to mind the going down by this time; you are getting to light on one foot or the other with considerable certainty. Six more attempts and six more falls make you perfect. You land in the saddle comfortably, next time, and stay there — that is, if you can be content to let your legs dangle, and leave the pedals alone a while; but if you grab at once for the pedals, you are gone again. You soon learn to wait a little and perfect your balance before reaching for the pedals; then the mounting-art is acquired, is complete, and a little practice will make it simple and easy to you, though spectators ought to keep off a rod or two to one side, along at first, if you have nothing against them.

And now you come to the voluntary dismount; you learned the other kind first of all. It is quite easy to tell one how to do the voluntary dismount; the words are few, the requirement simple, and apparently undifficult; let your left pedal go down till your left leg is nearly straight, turn your wheel to the left, and get off as you would from a horse. It certainly does sound exceedingly easy; but it isn't. I don't know why it isn't, but it isn't. Try as you may, you don't get down as you would from a horse, you get down as you would from a house afire. You make a spectacle of yourself every time.

II

During eight days I took a daily lesson of an hour and a half. At the end of this twelve working-hours' apprenticeship I was graduated — in the rough. I was pronounced competent to paddle my own bicycle without outside help. It seems incredible, this celerity of acquirement. It takes considerably longer than that to learn horseback-riding in the rough.

Now it is true that I could have learned without a teacher, but it would have been risky for me, because of my natural clumsiness. The self-taught man seldom knows anything accurately, and he does not know a tenth as much as he could have known if he had worked under teachers; and, besides, he brags, and is the means of fooling other thoughtless people into going and doing as he himself has done. There are those who imagine that the unlucky accidents of life — life's "experiences" — are in some way useful to us. I wish I could find out how. I never knew one of them to happen twice. They always change off and swap around and catch you on your inexperienced side. If personal experience can be worth anything as an education, it wouldn't seem likely that you could trip Methuselah; and yet if that old person could come back here it is more than likely that one of the first things he would do would be to take hold of one of these electric wires and tie himself all up in a knot. Now the surer thing and the wiser thing would be for him to ask somebody whether it was a good thing to take hold of. But that would not suit him; he would be one of the self-taught kind that go by experience; he would want to examine for himself. And he would find, for his instruction, that the coiled patriarch shuns the electric wire; and it would be useful to him, too, and would leave his education in quite a complete and rounded-out condition, till he should come again, some day, and go to bouncing a dynamite-can around to find out what was in it.

But we wander from the point. However, get a teacher; it saves much time and Pond's Extract.

Before taking final leave of me, my instructor inquired concerning my physical strength, and I was able to inform him that I hadn't any. He said that that was a defect which would make up-hill wheeling pretty difficult for me at first; but he also said the bicycle would soon remove it. The contrast between his muscles and mine was quite marked. He wanted to test mine, so I offered my biceps — which was my best. It almost made him smile. He said, "It is pulpy, and soft, and yielding, and rounded; it evades pressure, and glides from under the fingers; in the dark a body might think it was an oyster in a rag." Perhaps this made me look grieved, for he added, briskly: "Oh, that's all right; you needn't worry about that; in a little while you can't tell it from a petrified kidney. Just go right along with your practice; you're all right."

Then he left me, and I started out alone to seek adventures. You don't really have to seek them — that is nothing but a phrase — they come to you.

I chose a reposeful Sabbath-day sort of a back street which was about thirty yards wide between the curbstones. I knew it was not wide enough; still, I thought that by keeping strict watch and wasting no space unnecessarily I could crowd through.

Of course I had trouble mounting the machine, entirely on my own responsibility, with no encouraging moral support from the outside, no sympathetic instructor to say, "Good! now you're doing well — good again — don't hurry — there, now, you're all right —

—brace up, go ahead." In place of this I had some other support. This was a boy, who was perched on a gate-post munching a hunk of maple sugar.

He was full of interest and comment. The first time I failed and went down he said that if he was me he would dress up in pillows, that's what he would do. The next time I went down he advised me to go and learn to ride a tricycle first. The third time I collapsed he said he didn't believe I could stay on a horse-car. But next time I succeeded, and got clumsily under way in a weaving, tottering, uncertain fashion, and occupying pretty much all of the street. My slow and lumbering gait filled the boy to the chin with scorn, and he sung out, "My, but don't he rip along!" Then he got down from his post and loafed along the sidewalk, still observing and occasionally commenting. Presently he dropped into my wake and followed along behind. A little girl passed by, balancing a washboard on her head, and giggled, and seemed about to make a remark, but the boy said, rebukingly, "Let him alone, he's going to a funeral."

I had been familiar with that street for years, and had always supposed it was a dead level; but it was not, as the bicycle now informed me, to my surprise. The bicycle, in the hands of a novice, is as alert and acute as a spirit-level in the detecting of delicate and vanishing shades of difference in these matters. It notices a rise where your untrained eye would not observe that one existed; it notices any decline which water will run down. I was toiling up a slight rise, but was not aware of it. It made me tug and pant and perspire; and still, labor as I might, the machine came almost to a standstill every little while. At such times the boy would say: "That's it! take a rest — there ain't no hurry. They can't hold the funeral without *you*."

Stones were a bother to me. Even the smallest ones gave me a panic when I went over them. I could hit any kind of a stone, no matter how small, if I tried to miss it; and of course at first I couldn't help trying to do that. It is but natural. It is part of the ass that is put in us all, for some inscrutable reason.

I was at the end of my course, at last, and it was necessary for me to round to. This is not a pleasant thing, when you undertake it for the first time on your own responsibility, and neither is it likely to succeed. Your confidence oozes away, you fill steadily up with nameless apprehensions, every fiber of you is tense with a watchful strain, you start a cautious and gradual curve, but your squirmy nerves are all full of electric anxieties, so the curve is quickly demoralized into a jerky and perilous zigzag; then suddenly the nickel-clad horse takes the bit in its mouth and goes slanting for the curbstone, defying all prayers and all your powers to change its mind — your heart stands still, your breath hangs fire, your legs forget to work, straight on you go, and there are but a couple of feet between you and the curb now. And now is the desperate moment, the last chance to save yourself; of course all your instructions fly out of your head, and you whirl your wheel *away* from the curb instead of *toward* it, and so you go sprawling on that granite-bound inhospitable shore. That was my luck; that was my experience. I dragged myself out from under the indestructible bicycle and sat down on the curb to examine.

I started on the return trip. It was now that I saw a farmer's wagon poking along down toward me, loaded with cabbages. If I needed anything to perfect the precariousness of my steering, it was just that. The farmer was occupying the middle of the road with his wagon, leaving barely fourteen or fifteen yards of space on either side. I couldn't shout at him — a beginner can't shout; if he opens his mouth he is gone; he must keep all his attention on his business. But in this grisly emergency, the boy came to the rescue, and for once I had to be grateful to him. He kept a sharp lookout on the swiftly varying impulses and inspirations of my bicycle, and shouted to the man accordingly:

"To the left! Turn to the left, or this jackass'll run over you!" The man started to do it. "No, to the right, to the right! Hold on! *that* won't do! — to the left! — to the right! — to the *left!* — right! left — ri — Stay where you *are*, or you're a goner!"

And just then I caught the off horse in the starboard and went down in a pile. I said, "Hang it! Couldn't you *see* I was coming?"

"Yes, I see you was coming, but I couldn't tell which *way* you was coming. Nobody could — now, *could* they? You couldn't yourself — now, *could* you? So what could *I* do?"

There was something in that, and so I had the magnanimity to say so. I said I was no doubt as much to blame as he was.

Within the next five days I achieved so much progress that the boy couldn't keep up with me. He had to go back to his gate-post, and content himself with watching me fall at long range.

There was a row of low stepping-stones across one end of the street, a measured yard apart. Even after I got so I could steer pretty fairly I was so afraid of those stones that I always hit them. They gave me the worst falls I ever got in that street, except those which I got from dogs. I have seen it stated that no expert is quick enough to run over a dog; that a dog is always able to skip out of his way. I think that that may be true; but I think that the reason he couldn't run over the dog was because he was trying to. I did not try to run over any dog. But I ran over every dog that came along. I think it makes a great deal of difference. If you try to run over the dog he knows how to calculate, but if you are trying to miss him he does not know how to calculate, and is liable to jump the wrong way every time. It was always so in my experience. Even when I could not hit a wagon I could hit a dog that came to see me practise. They all liked to see me practise, and they all came, for there was very little going on in our neighborhood to entertain a dog. It took time to learn to miss a dog, but I achieved even that.

I can steer as well as I want to, now, and I will catch that boy out one of these days and run over *him* if he doesn't reform.

Get a bicycle. You will not regret it, if you live.

JOURNALISM IN TENNESSEE

The editor of the Memphis *Avalanche* swoops thus mildly down upon a correspondent who posted him as a Radical: — "While he was writing the first word, the middle, dotting his i's, crossing his t's, and punching his period, he knew he was concocting a sentence that was saturated with infamy and reeking with falsehood." — *Exchange.*

I was told by the physician that a Southern climate would improve my health, and so I went down to Tennessee, and got a berth on the *Morning Glory and Johnson County War-Whoop* as associate editor. When I went on duty I found the chief editor sitting tilted back in a three-legged chair with his feet on a pine table. There was another pine table in the room and another afflicted chair, and both were half buried under newspapers and scraps and sheets of manuscript. There was a wooden box of sand, sprinkled with cigar stubs and "old soldiers," and a stove with a door hanging by its upper hinge. The chief editor had a long-tailed black cloth frock coat on, and white linen pants. His boots were small and neatly blacked. He wore a ruffled shirt, a large seal ring, a standing collar of obsolete pattern, and a checkered neckerchief with the ends hanging down. Date of costume about 1848. He was smoking a cigar, and trying to think of a word, and in pawing his hair he had rumpled his locks a good deal. He was scowling fearfully, and I judged that he was concocting a particularly knotty editorial. He told me to take the exchanges and skim through them and write up the "Spirit of the Tennessee Press," condensing into the article all of their contents that seemed of interest. I wrote as follows: —

SPIRIT OF THE TENNESSEE PRESS

THE EDITORS of the *Semi-Weekly Earthquake* evidently labor under a misapprehension with regard to the Ballyhack railroad. It is not the object of the company to leave Buzzardville off to one side. On the contrary, they consider it one of the most important points along the line, and consequently can have no desire to slight it. The gentlemen of the *Earthquake* will, of course, take pleasure in making the correction.

John W. Blossom, Esq., the able editor of the Higginsville *Thunderbolt and Battle Cry of Freedom*, arrived in the city yesterday. He is stopping at the Van Buren House.

We observe that our contemporary of the Mud Springs *Morning Howl* has fallen into the error of supposing that the election of Van Werter is not an established fact, but he will have discovered his mistake before this reminder reaches him, no doubt. He was doubtless misled by incomplete election returns.

It is pleasant to note that the city of Blathersville is endeavoring to contract with some New York gentlemen to pave its well-nigh impassable streets with the Nicholson pavement. The *Daily Hurrah* urges the measure with ability, and seems confident of ultimate success.

I passed my manuscript over to the chief editor for acceptance, alteration, or destruction. He glanced at it and his face clouded. He ran his eye down the pages, and his countenance grew portentous. It was easy to see that something was wrong. Presently he sprang up and said —

"Thunder and lightning! Do you suppose I am going to speak of those cattle that way? Do you suppose my subscribers are going to stand such gruel as that? Give me the pen!"

I never saw a pen scrape and scratch its way so viciously, or plough through another man's verbs and adjectives so relentlessly. While he was in the midst of his work, somebody shot at him through the open window, and marred the symmetry of my ear.

"Ah," said he, "that is that scoundrel Smith, of the *Moral Volcano* — he was due yesterday." And he snatched a navy revolver from his belt and fired. Smith dropped, shot in the thigh. The shot spoiled Smith's aim, who was just taking a second chance, and he crippled a stranger. It was me. Merely a finger shot off.

Then the chief editor went on with his erasures and interlineations. Just as he finished them a hand-grenade came down the stove pipe, and the explosion shivered the stove into a thousand fragments. However, it did no further damage, except that a vagrant piece knocked a couple of my teeth out.

"That stove is utterly ruined," said the chief editor.

I said I believed it was.

"Well, no matter — don't want it this kind of weather. I know the man that did it. I'll get him. Now, *here* is the way this stuff ought to be written."

I took the manuscript. It was scarred with erasures and interlineations till its mother wouldn't have known it if it had had one. It now read as follows:—

SPIRIT OF THE TENNESSEE PRESS

THE INVETERATE liars of the *Semi-Weekly Earthquake* are evidently endeavoring to palm off upon a noble and chivalrous people another of their vile and brutal falsehoods with regard to that most glorious conception of the nineteenth century, the Ballyhack railroad. The idea that Buzzardville was to be left off at one side originated in their own fulsome brains — or rather in the settlings which *they* regard as brains. They had better swallow this lie if they want to save their abandoned reptile carcasses the cowhiding they so richly deserve.

That ass, Blossom, of the Higginsville *Thunderbolt and Battle Cry of Freedom*, is down here again sponging at the Van Buren.

We observe that the besotted blackguard of the Mud Springs *Morning Howl* is giving out, with its usual propensity for lying, that Van

Werter is not elected. The heaven-born mission of journalism is to disseminate truth; to eradicate error; to educate, refine and elevate the tone of public morals and manners, and make all men more gentle, more virtuous, more charitable, and in all ways better, and holier, and happier; and yet this black-hearted scoundrel degrades his great office persistently to the dissemination of falsehood, calumny, vituperation, and vulgarity.

Blathersville wants a Nicholson pavement — it wants a jail and poorhouse more. The idea of a pavement in a one horse town composed of two gin mills, a blacksmith's shop, and that mustard-plaster of a newspaper, the *Daily Hurrah!* The crawling insect, Buckner, who edits the *Hurrah,* is braying about this business with his customary imbecility, and imagining that he is talking sense.

"Now *that* is the way to write — peppery and to the point. Mush-and-milk journalism gives me the fantods."

About this time a brick came through the window with a splintering crash, and gave me a considerable of a jolt in the back. I moved out of range — I began to feel in the way.

The chief said, "That was the Colonel, likely. I've been expecting him for two days. He will be up, now, right away."

He was correct. The Colonel appeared in the door a moment afterward with a dragoon revolver in his hand.

He said, "Sir, have I the honor of addressing the poltroon who edits this mangy sheet?"

"You have. Be seated, sir. Be careful of the chair, one of its legs is gone. I believe I have the honor of addressing the putrid liar, Col. Blatherskite Tecumseh?"

"Right, sir. I have a little account to settle with you. If you are at leisure we will begin."

"I have an article on the 'Encouraging Progress of Moral and Intellectual Development in America' to finish, but there is no hurry. Begin."

Both pistols rang out their fierce clamor at the same instant. The chief lost a lock of his hair, and the Colonel's bullet ended its career in the fleshy part of my thigh. The Colonel's left shoulder was clipped a little. They fired again. Both missed their men this time, but I got my share, a shot in the arm. At the third fire both gentlemen were wounded slightly, and I had a knuckle chipped. I then said, I believed I would go out and take a walk, as this was a private matter, and I had a delicacy about participating in it further. But both gentlemen begged me to keep my seat, and assured me that I was not in the way.

They then talked about the elections and the

crops while they reloaded, and I fell to tying up my wounds. But presently they opened fire again with animation, and every shot took effect — but it is proper to remark that five out of the six fell to my share. The sixth one mortally wounded the Colonel, who remarked, with fine humor, that he would have to say good morning now, as he had business up town. He then inquired the way to the undertaker's and left.

The chief turned to me and said, "I am expecting company to dinner, and shall have to get ready. It will be a favor to me if you will read proof and attend to the customers."

I winced a little at the idea of attending to the customers, but I was too bewildered by the fusillade that was still ringing in my ears to think of anything to say.

He continued, "Jones will be here at 3 — cowhide him. Gillespie will call earlier, perhaps — throw him out of the window. Ferguson will be along about 4 — kill him. That is all for to-day, I believe. If you have any odd time, you may write a blistering article on the police — give the Chief Inspector rats. The cowhides are under the table; weapons in the drawer — ammunition there in the corner — lint and bandages up there in the pigeon-holes. In case of accident, go to Lancet, the surgeon, down-stairs. He advertises — we take it out in trade."

He was gone. I shuddered. At the end of the next three hours I had been through perils so awful that all peace of mind and all cheerfulness were gone from me. Gillespie had called and thrown *me* out of the window. Jones arrived promptly, and when I got ready to do the cow-hiding he took the job off my hands. In an encounter with a stranger, not in the bill of fare, I had lost my scalp. Another stranger, by the name of Thompson, left me a mere wreck and ruin of chaotic rags. And at last, at bay in the corner, and beset by an infuriated mob of editors, black-legs, politicians, and desperadoes, who raved and swore and flourished their weapons about my head till the air shimmered with glancing flashes of steel, I was in the act of resigning my berth on the paper when the chief arrived, and with him a rabble of charmed and enthusiastic friends. Then ensued a scene of riot and carnage such as no human pen, or steel one either, could describe. People were shot, probed, dismembered, blown up, thrown out of the window. There was a brief tornado of murky blasphemy, with a confused and frantic war-dance glimmering through it, and then all was over. In five minutes there was silence, and the gory chief and I sat alone and surveyed the sanguinary ruin that strewed the floor around us.

He said, "You'll like this place when you get used to it."

I said, "I'll have to get you to excuse me; I think maybe I might write to suit you after a while; as soon as I had had some practice and learned the language I am confident I could. But, to speak the plain truth, that sort of energy of expression has its inconveniences, and a man is liable to interruptions. You see that yourself. Vigorous writing is calculated to elevate the public, no doubt, but then I do not like to attract so much attention as it calls forth. I can't write with comfort when I am interrupted so much as I have been to-day. I like this berth well enough, but I don't like to be left here to wait on the customers. The experiences are novel, I grant you, and entertaining too, after a fashion, but they are not judiciously distributed. A gentleman shoots at you through the window and cripples *me*; a bomb-shell comes down the stove-pipe for your gratification and sends the stove-door down *my* throat; a friend drops in to swap compliments with you, and freckles *me* with bullet-holes till my skin won't hold my principles; you go to dinner, and Jones comes with his cowhide, Gillespie throws me out of the window, Thompson tears all my clothes off, and an entire stranger takes my scalp with the easy freedom of an old acquaintance; and in less than five minutes all the blackguards in the country arrive in their war-paint, and proceed to scare the rest of me to death with their tomahawks. Take it altogether, I never had such a spirited time in all my life as I have had to-day. No; I like you, and I like your calm unruffled way of explaining things to the customers, but you see I am not used to it. The Southern heart is too impulsive; Southern hospitality is too lavish with the stranger. The paragraphs which I have written to-day, and into whose cold sentences your masterly hand has infused the fervent spirit of Tennessean journalism, will wake up another nest of hornets. All that mob of editors will come — and they will come hungry, too, and want somebody for breakfast. I shall have to bid you adieu. I decline to be present at these festivities. I came South for my health, I will go back on the same errand, and suddenly. Tennessean journalism is too stirring for me."

After which we parted with mutual regret, and I took apartments at the hospital.

CANNIBALISM IN THE CARS

I VISITED St. Louis lately, and on my way west, after changing cars at Terre Haute, Indiana, a mild, benevolent-looking gentleman of about forty-five, or may be fifty, came in at one of the way-stations and sat down beside me. We talked together pleasantly on various subjects for an hour, perhaps, and I found him exceedingly intelligent and entertaining. When he learned that I was from Washington, he immediately began to ask questions about various public men, and about Congressional affairs; and I saw very shortly that I was conversing with a man who was perfectly familiar with the ins and outs of political life at the Capital, even to the ways and manners, and customs of procedure of Senators and Representatives in the chambers of the National Legislature. Presently two men halted near us for a single moment, and one said to the other:

"Harris, if you'll do that for me, I'll never forget you, my boy."

My new comrade's eyes lighted pleasantly. The words had touched upon a happy memory, I thought. Then his face settled into thoughtfulness — almost into gloom. He turned to me and said, "Let me tell you a story; let me give you a secret chapter of my life — a chapter that has never been referred to by me since its events transpired. Listen patiently, and promise that you will not interrupt me."

I said I would not, and he related the following strange adventure, speaking sometimes with animation, sometimes with melancholy, but always with feeling and earnestness.

ON THE 19th of December, 1853, I started from St. Louis on the evening train bound for Chicago. There were only twenty-four passengers, all told. There were no ladies and no children. We were in excellent spirits, and pleasant acquaintanceships were formed. The journey bade fair to be a happy one; and no individual in the party, I think, had even the vaguest presentment of the horrors we were soon to undergo.

At 11 P.M. it began to snow hard. Shortly after leaving the small village of Welden, we entered upon that tremendous prairie solitude that stretches its leagues on leagues of houseless dreariness far away towards the Jubilee Settlements. The winds, unobstructed by trees or hills, or even vagrant rocks, whistled fiercely across the level desert, driving the falling snow before it like spray from the crested waves of a stormy sea. The snow was deepening fast; and we knew, by the diminished speed of the train, that the engine was ploughing through it with steadily increasing difficulty. Indeed, it almost came to a dead halt sometimes, in the midst of great drifts that piled themselves like colossal graves across the track. Conversation began to flag. Cheerfulness gave place to grave concern. The possibility of being imprisoned in the snow, on the bleak prairie, fifty miles from any house, presented itself to every mind, and extended its depressing influence over every spirit.

At two o'clock in the morning I was aroused out of an uneasy slumber by the ceasing of all motion about me. The appalling truth flashed upon me instantly — we were captives in a snow-drift! "All hands to the rescue!" Every man sprang to obey. Out into the wild night, the pitchy darkness, the billowy snow, the driving storm, every soul leaped, with the consciousness that a moment lost now might bring destruction to us all. Shovels, hands, boards —anything, everything that could displace snow, was brought into instant requisition. It was a weird picture, that small company of frantic men fighting the banking snows, half in the blackest shadow and half in the angry light of the locomotive's reflector.

One short hour sufficed to prove the utter uselessness of our efforts. The storm barricaded the track with a dozen drifts while we dug one away. And worse than this, it was discovered that the last grand charge the engine had made upon the enemy had broken the fore-and-aft shaft of the driving-wheel! With a free track before us we should still have been helpless. We entered the car wearied with labor, and very sorrowful. We gathered about the stoves, and gravely canvassed our situation. We had no provisions whatever — in this lay our chief distress. We could not freeze, for there was a good supply of wood in the tender. This was our only comfort. The discussion ended at last in accepting the disheartening decision of the conductor, viz., that it would be death for any man to attempt to travel fifty miles on foot through snow like that. We could not send for help; and even if we could, it could not come. We must submit, and await, as patiently as we might, succor or starvation! I think the stoutest heart there felt a momentary chill when those words were uttered.

Within the hour conversation subsided to a low murmur here and there about the car, caught fitfully between the rising and falling of the blast; the lamps grew dim; and the majority of the castaways settled themselves among the flickering shadows to think — to forget the present, if they could — to sleep, if they might.

The eternal night — it surely seemed eternal to us — wore its lagging hours away at last, and the cold grey dawn broke in the east. As the light grew stronger the passengers began to stir and give signs of life, one after another, and each in turn pushed his slouched hat up from his forehead, stretched his stiffened limbs, and glanced out at the windows upon the cheerless prospect. It was cheerless indeed! — not a living thing visible anywhere, not a human habitation; nothing but a vast white desert; uplifted sheets of snow drifting hither and thither before the wind — a world of eddying flakes shutting out the firmament above.

All day we moped about the cars, saying little, thinking much. Another lingering dreary night — and hunger.

Another dawning — another day of silence, sadness, wasting hunger, hopeless watching for succor that could not come. A night of restless slumber, filled with dreams of feasting — wakings distressed with the gnawings of hunger.

The fourth day came and went — and the fifth! Five days of dreadful imprisonment! A savage hunger looked out at every eye. There was in it a sign of awful import — the foreshadowing of a something that was vaguely shaping itself in every heart — a something which no tongue dared yet to frame into words.

The sixth day passed — the seventh dawned upon as gaunt and haggard and hopeless a company of men as ever stood in the shadow of death. It must out now! That thing which had been growing up in every heart was ready to leap from every lip at last! Nature had been taxed to the utmost — she must yield. RICHARD H. GASTON, of Minnesota, tall, cadaverous, and pale, rose up. All knew what was coming. All prepared — every emotion, every semblance of excitement was smothered — only a calm, thoughtful seriousness appeared in the eyes that were lately so wild.

"Gentlemen, — It cannot be delayed longer! The time is at hand! We must determine which of us shall die to furnish food for the rest!"

Mr. JOHN J. WILLIAMS, of Illinois, rose and

said: "Gentlemen, — I nominate the Rev. James Sawyer, of Tennessee."

Mr. WM. R. ADAMS, of Indiana, said: "I nominate Mr. Daniel Slote, of New York."

Mr. CHARLES J. LANGDON: "I nominate Mr. Samuel A. Bowen, of St. Louis."

Mr. SLOTE: "Gentlemen, — I desire to decline in favor of Mr. John A. Van Nostrand, Jun., of New Jersey."

Mr. GASTON: "If there be no objection, the gentleman's desire will be acceded to."

Mr. VAN NOSTRAND objecting, the resignation of Mr. Slote was rejected. The resignations of Messrs. Sawyer and Bowen were also offered, and refused upon the same grounds.

Mr. A.L. BASCOM, of Ohio: "I move that the nominations now close, and that the House proceed to an election by ballot."

Mr. SAWYER: "Gentlemen, — I protest earnestly against these proceedings. They are, in every way, irregular and unbecoming. I must beg to move that they be dropped at once, and that we elect a chairman of the meeting and proper officers to assist him, and then we can go on with the business before us understandingly."

Mr. BELL, of Iowa: "Gentlemen, — I object. This is no time to stand upon forms and ceremonious observances. For more than seven days we have been without food. Every moment we lose in idle discussion increases our distress. I am satisfied with the nominations that have been made — every gentleman present is, I believe — and I, for one, do not see why we should not proceed at once to elect one or more of them. I wish to offer a resolution —"

Mr. GASTON: "It would be objected to, and have to lie over one day under the rules, thus bringing about the very delay you wish to avoid. The gentleman from New Jersey —"

Mr. VAN NOSTRAND: "Gentlemen, — I am a stranger among you; I have not sought the distinction that has been conferred upon me, and I feel a delicacy —"

Mr. MORGAN, of Alabama (interrupting): "I move the previous question."

The motion was carried, and further debate shut off, of course. The motion to elect officers was passed, and under it Mr. Gaston was chosen chairman, Mr. Blake secretary, Messrs. Holcomb, Dyer, and Baldwin, a committee on nominations, and Mr. R.M. Howland, purveyor, to assist the committee in making selections.

A recess of half an hour was then taken, and some little caucussing followed. At the sound of the gavel the meeting reassembled, and the committee reported in favor of Messrs. George Ferguson, of Kentucky, Lucien Herrman, of Louisiana, and W. Messick, of Colorado, as candidates. The report was accepted.

Mr. ROGERS, of Missouri: "Mr. President, — The report being properly before the House now, I move to amend it by substituting for the name of Mr. Herrman that of Mr. Lucius Harris, of St. Louis, who is well and honorably known to us all. I do not wish to be understood as casting the least reflection upon the high character and standing of the gentleman from Louisiana — far from it. I respect and esteem him as much as any gentleman here present possibly can; but none of us can be blind to the fact that he has lost more flesh during the week that we have lain here than any among us — none of us can be blind to the fact that the committee has been derelict to its duty, either through negligence or a graver fault, in thus offering for our suffrages a gentleman who, however pure his own motives may be, has really less nutriment in him —"

THE CHAIR: "The gentleman from Missouri will take his seat. The Chair cannot allow the integrity of the Committee to be questioned save by the regular course, under the rules. What action will the House take upon the gentleman's motion?"

Mr. HALLIDAY, of Virginia: "I move to further amend the report by substituting Mr. Harvey Davis, of Oregon, for Mr. Messick. It may be urged by gentlemen that the hardships and privations of a frontier life have rendered Mr. Davis tough; but, gentlemen, is this a time to cavil at toughness? is this a time to be fastidious concerning trifles? is this a time to dispute about matters of paltry significance? No, gentlemen, bulk is what we desire — substance, weight, bulk — these are the supreme requisites now — not talent, not genius, not education. I insist upon my motion.''

Mr. MORGAN (excitedly): "Mr. Chairman, — I do most strenuously object to this amendment. The gentleman from Oregon is old, and furthermore is bulky only in bone — not in flesh. I ask the gentleman from Virginia if it is soup we want instead of solid sustenance? if he would delude us with shadows? if he would mock our suffering with an Oregonial spectre? I ask him if he can look upon the anxious faces around him, if he can gaze into our sad eyes, if he can listen to the beating of our expectant hearts, and still thrust this famine-stricken fraud upon us! I ask him if he can think of our desolate state, of our past sorrows, of our dark future, and still unpityingly foist upon us this wreck, this ruin, this tottering swindle, this gnarled and blighted and sapless vagabond from Oregon's inhospitable shores? Never!'' (Applause.)

The amendment was put to vote, after a fiery debate, and lost. Mr. Harris was substituted on the first amendment. The balloting then began. Five ballots were held without a choice. On the sixth, Mr. Harris was elected, all voting for him but himself. It was then moved that his election should be ratified by acclamation, which was lost, in consequence of his again voting against himself.

Mr. RADWAY moved that the House now take up the remaining candidates, and go into an election for breakfast. This was carried.

On the first ballot there was a tie, half the members favoring one candidate on acount of his youth, and half favoring the other on account of his superior size. The President gave the casting vote for the latter, Mr. Messick. This decision created considerable dissatisfaction among the friends of Mr. Ferguson, the defeated candidate, and there was some talk of demanding a new ballot; but in the midst of it, a motion to adjourn was carried, and the meeting broke up at once.

The preparations for supper diverted the attention of the Ferguson faction from the discussion of their grievance for a long time, and then, when they would have taken it up again, the happy announcement that Mr. Harris was ready, drove all thought of it to the winds.

We improvised tables by propping up the backs of car-seats, and sat down with hearts full of gratitude to the finest supper that had blessed our vision for seven torturing days. How changed we were from what we had been a few short hours before! Hopeless, sad-eyed misery, hunger, feverish anxiety, desperation, then — thankfulness, serenity, joy too deep for utterance now. That I know was the cheeriest hour of my eventful life. The winds howled, and blew the snow wildly about our prison-house, but they were powerless to distress us any more. I liked Harris. He might have been better done, perhaps, but I am free to say that no man ever agreed with me better than Harris, or afforded me so large a degree of satisfaction. Messick was very well, though rather high-flavored, but for genuine nutritiousness and delicacy of fibre, give me Harris. Messick had his good points — I will not attempt to deny it, nor do I wish to do it — but he was no more fitted for breakfast than a mummy would be, sir — not a bit. Lean? — why, bless me! — and tough? Ah, he was very tough! You could not imagine it, — you could never imagine anything like it."

"Do you mean to tell me that —"

"Do not interrupt me, please."

After breakfast we elected a man by the name of Walker, from Detroit, for supper. He was very good. I wrote his wife so afterwards. He was worthy of all praise. I shall always remember Walker. He was a little rare, but very good. And then the next morning we had Mor-

gan, of Alabama, for breakfast. He was one of
the finest men I ever sat down to,—handsome,
educated, refined, spoke several languages
fluently — a perfect gentleman — he was a perfect gentleman, and singularly juicy. For supper
we had that Oregon patriarch, and he *was* a
fraud, there is no question about it — old,
scraggy, tough, nobody can picture the reality. I
finally said, gentlemen, you can do as you like,
but *I* will wait for another election. And
Grimes, of Illinois, said, "Gentlemen, *I* will
wait also. When you elect a man that has *something* to recommend him, I shall be glad to join
you again." It soon became evident that there
was general dissatisfaction with Davis, of
Oregon, and so, to preserve the good-will that
had prevailed so pleasantly since we had had
Harris, an election was called, and the result of
it was that Baker, of Georgia, was chosen. He
was splendid! Well, well — after that we had
Doolittle and Hawkins, and McElroy (there
was some complaint about McElroy, because
he was uncommonly short and thin), and Pen-
rod, and two Smiths, and Bailey (Bailey had a
wooden leg, which was clear loss, but he was
otherwise good), and an Indian boy, and an
organ grinder, and a gentleman by the name of
Buckminster — a poor stick of a vagabond that
wasn't any good for company and no account
for breakfast. We were glad we got him elected

before relief came.

"And so the blessed relief *did* come at last?"

"Yes, it came one bright, sunny morning, just after election. John Murphy was the choice, and there never was a better, I am willing to testify; but John Murphy came home with us, in the train that came to succor us, and lived to marry the widow Harris —"

"Relict of —"

"Relict of our first choice. He married her, and is happy and respected and prosperous yet. Ah, it was like a novel, sir — it was like a romance. This is my stopping-place, sir; I must bid you good-bye. Any time that you can make it convenient to tarry a day or two with me, I shall be glad to have you. I like you, sir; I have conceived an affection for you. I could like you as well as I liked Harris himself, sir. Good day, sir, and a pleasant journey."

He was gone. I never felt so stunned, so distressed, so bewildered in my life. But in my soul I was glad he was gone. With all his gentleness of manner and his soft voice, I shuddered whenever he turned his hungry eye upon me; and when I heard that I had achieved his perilous affection, and that I stood almost with the late Harris in his esteem, my heart fairly stood still!

I was bewildered beyond description. I did not doubt his word; I could not question a single item in a statement so stamped with the earnestness of truth as his; but its dreadful details overpowered me, and threw my thoughts into hopeless confusion. I saw the conductor looking at me. I said, "Who is that man?"

"He was a member of Congress once, and a good one. But he got caught in a snowdrift in the cars, and like to been starved to death. He got so frost-bitten and frozen up generally, and used up for want of something to eat, that he was sick and out of his head two or three months afterwards. He is all right now, only he is a monomaniac, and when he gets on that old subject he never stops till he has eat up that whole car-load of people he talks about. He would have finished the crowd by this time, only he had to get out here. He has got their names as pat as A, B, C. When he gets them all eat up but himself, he always says: — 'Then the hour for the usual election for breakfast having arrived, and there being no opposition, I was duly elected, after which, there being no objections offered, I resigned. Thus I am here.'"

I felt inexpressibly relieved to know that I had only been listening to the harmless vagaries of a madman instead of the genuine experiences of a bloodthirsty cannibal.